A Year of Beasts

ASHLEY WOLFF
A Year of Beasts

E. P. DUTTON   NEW YORK

Copyright © 1986 by Ashley Wolff

All rights reserved.

Library of Congress Cataloging in Publication Data
Wolff, Ashley.
   A year of beasts.
   Summary: Ellie and Peter see many different field and forest
animals around their country house throughout the year.
   [1. Animals—Fiction.   2. Seasons—Fiction.
3. Country life—Fiction]   I. Title.
PZ7.W821234Ye   1986   [E]   85-27419
ISBN 0-525-44240-5

Published in the United States by E. P. Dutton,
2 Park Avenue, New York, N.Y. 10016
Published simultaneously in Canada by
Fitzhenry & Whiteside Limited, Toronto

Editor: Donna Brooks   Designer: Riki Levinson
Printed in Hong Kong by South China Printing Co.
First Edition   W   10 9 8 7 6 5 4 3 2 1

for Donna

In winter, in spring
in summer, and in fall—
in every month of the year
beasts of all kinds
live in the fields and forests
around Ellie and
Peter's house.

White-tailed deer in January

Red foxes in February

A woodchuck in March

Cottontail rabbits in April

Otters in May

Skunks and cows in June

Chipmunks in July

Beavers in August

Field mice in September

A porcupine in October

Raccoons in November

Squirrels, deer,

and a rabbit in December